DREAM DOODLE DRAW!
Under the Sea

by Sonali Fry
Illustrated by Migy Blanco

LITTLE SIMON
New York London Toronto Sydney New Delhi

The doodles in this book were created by

Alexandria Janke 201622
fora Birtha her 8th pesent

LITTLE SIMON

An imprint of Simon & Schuster Children's Publishing Division

1230 Avenue of the Americas, New York, New York 10020

For information about special discounts for bulk purchases, please contact Simon & Schuster Special Sales

at 1-866-506-1949 or business@simonandschuster.com.

The Simon & Schuster Speakers Bureau can bring authors to your live event. For more information or to book an event contact the

Simon & Schuster Speakers Bureau at 1-866-248-3049 or visit our website at www.simonspeakers.com.

Manufactured in China 0214 SCP

First Edition

2   4   6   8   10   9   7   5   3   1

ISBN 978-1-4814-0453-2

Get ready to dive in to the world under the sea!

Doodle some faces onto these sea stars!

This orca is dreaming about something yummy.

Draw your favorite treat in his thought bubble!

Decorate these shells with stripes, swirls, and polka dots!

Start

This big blue whale is
looking for her baby!
Can you help her
find him?

Finish

These fish have found an anchor!
Draw the ship that dropped it.

Can you spot these images in the scene?

Color them in!

Ooh! A message in a bottle!

What do you think the message said?
Write it here.

Fill these pages with all kinds of fish!

Two friendly dolphins are bouncing with the waves.

Draw two more on this page!

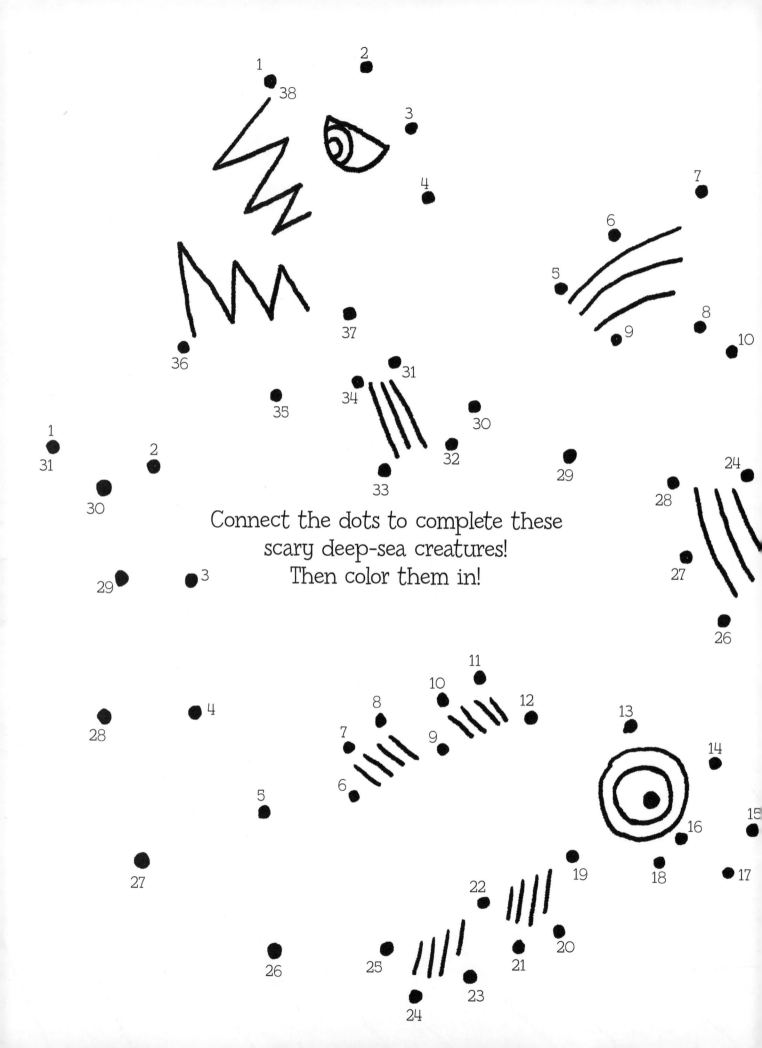

Connect the dots to complete these
scary deep-sea creatures!
Then color them in!

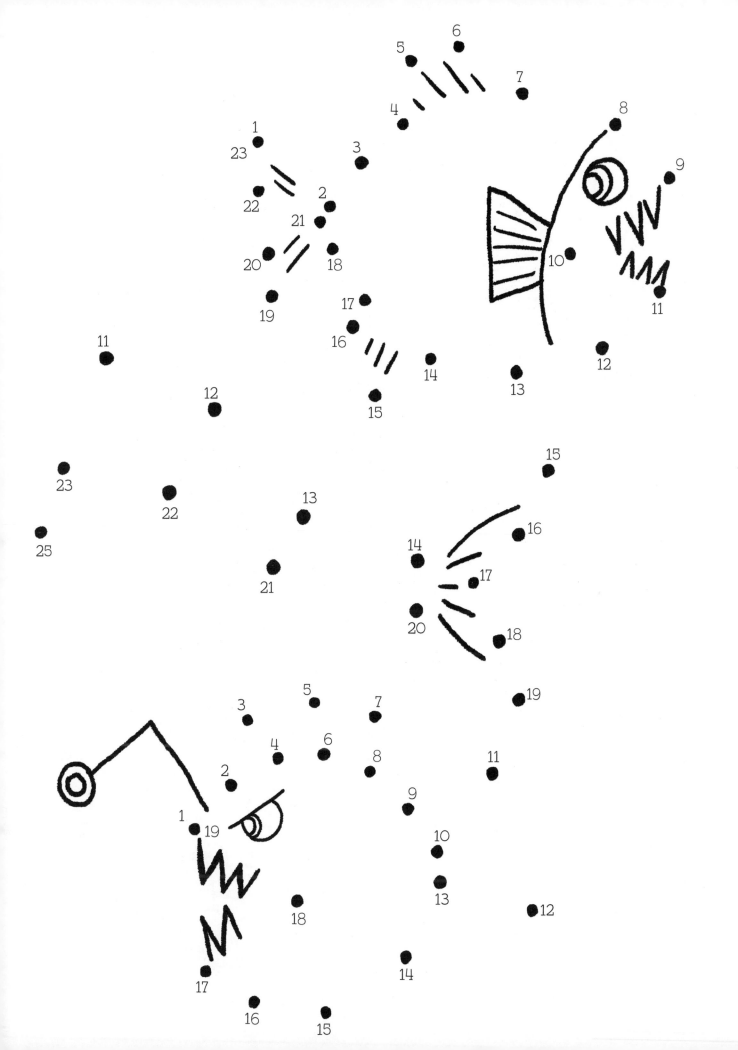

Eek! These waters are filled with eels!

Doodle your own eels on this page.

Doodle some patterns onto these turtles' shells!

A submarine is exploring the bottom of the sea.
What does it see?

Draw some googly eyes on these crabs!

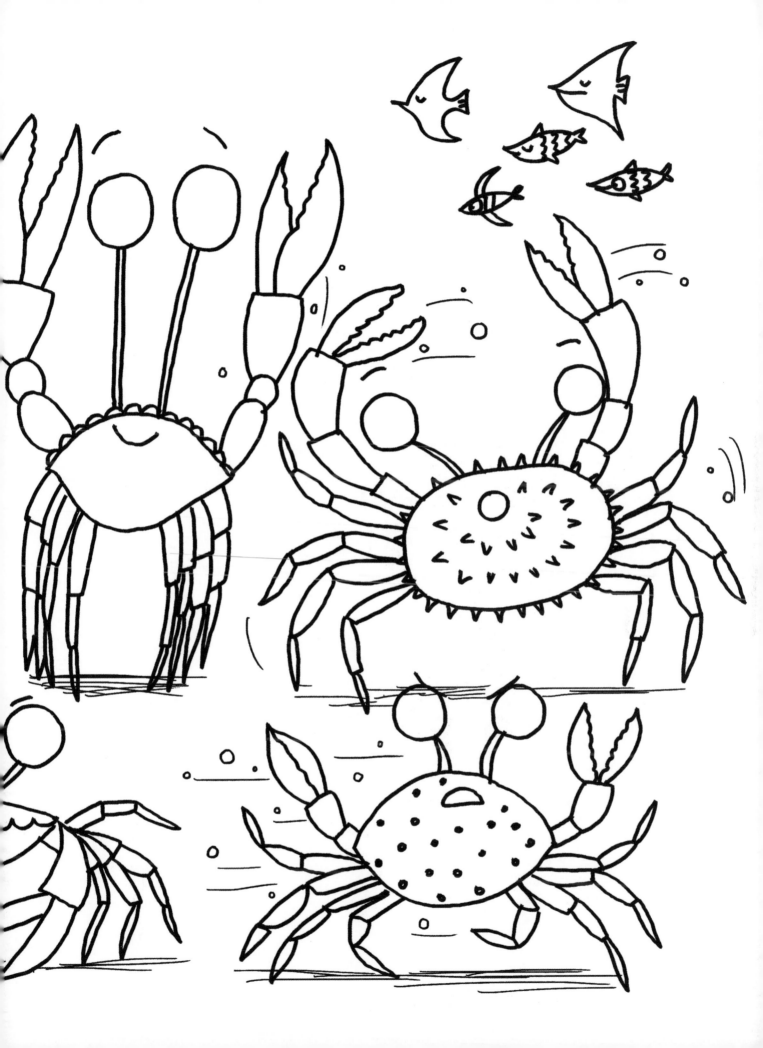

Yikes! This barracuda is chasing some angelfish.

Draw some rocks between them
to keep the angelfish safe!

These baby turtles are making their way
toward the ocean.

Draw the shoreline so they can see
how far they have to go!

These sea horses are resting on sea grasses and coral.
Use your favorite colors to fill in these pages.

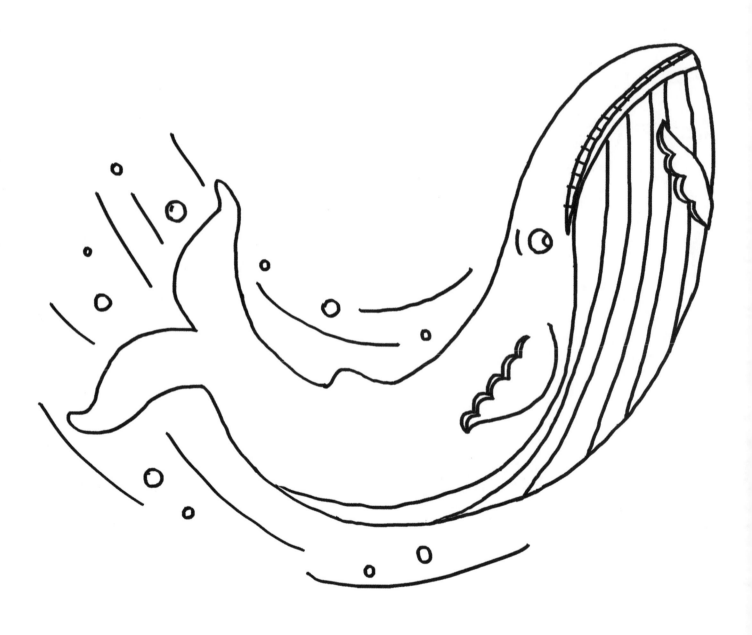

This blue whale is looking for some lunch.

What do you think he wants to eat?
Draw it here.

What is slithering out from under the rocks?
It's an __ __ __ !
Fill up the rest of this page any way you wish!

Color in these sea urchins!

Draw the other half of this octopus!

Connect the dots to create some sea turtles.
Now color them in any way you like!

Draw your own unique fish!

What would you name it? Write the name on the line.

_____

A diver is looking for
some buried treasure!
Can you help him find it?

Start

Finish

Now fill the treasure chest with jewels!

If you could dream up your own undersea world,
what would it look like?
Draw it for everyone to see!

These two fish are kissing!
Draw a heart made out of bubbles around them!

Can you spot the hammerhead shark? Color it in!

Some creatures are swimming across the ocean floor.
Connect the dots to find out what they are!

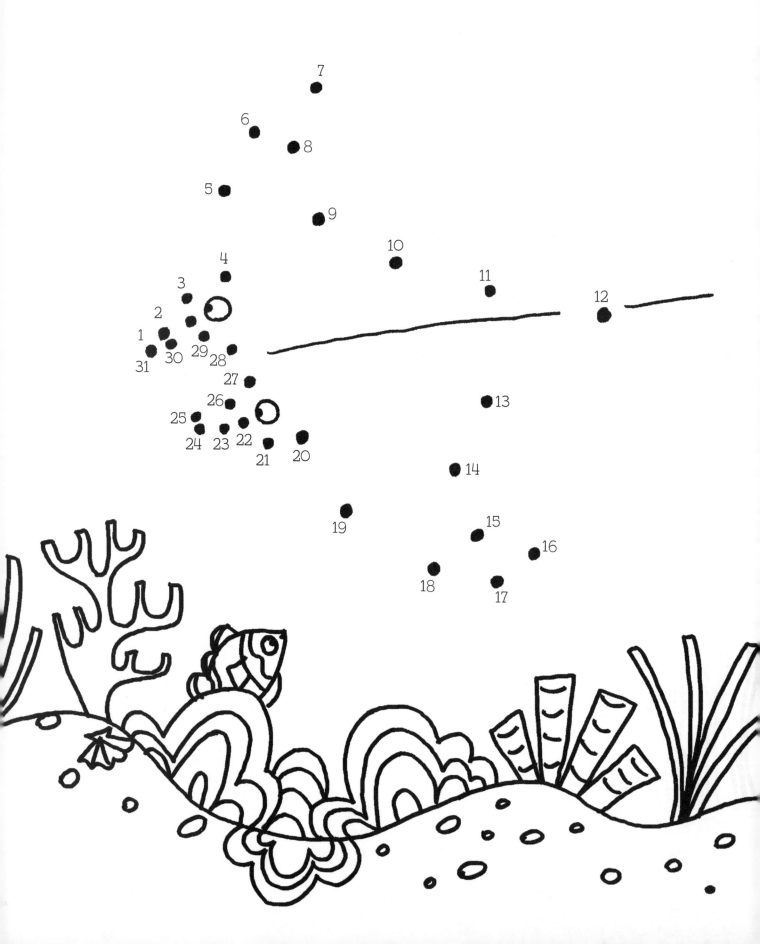

They are manta rays!

These snorkelers are looking for some colorful fish.
Add them to the scene!

Draw what's above and below sea level.

Create your own seashells!

Doodle two silly sea creatures!

Now give them names!

_____   _____

Add some colors and patterns to this coral.

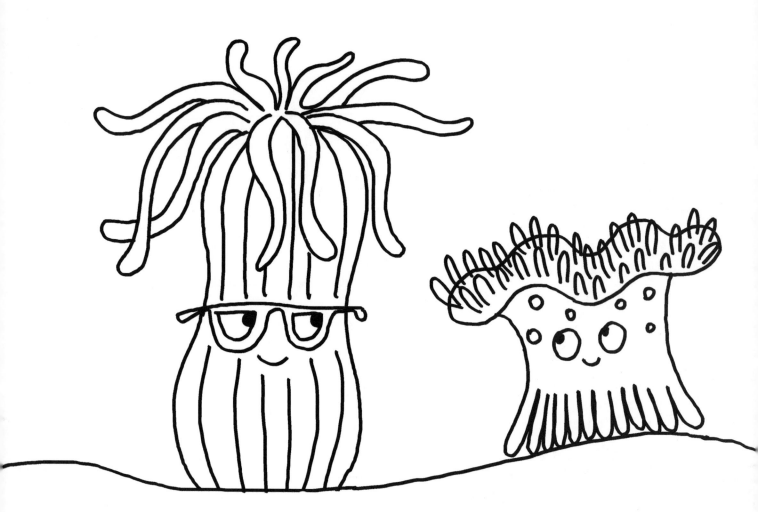

These sea anemones sway back and forth in the water.
Add a few more sea anemones to the scene!

Do you see these objects in this scene?

Color them in!

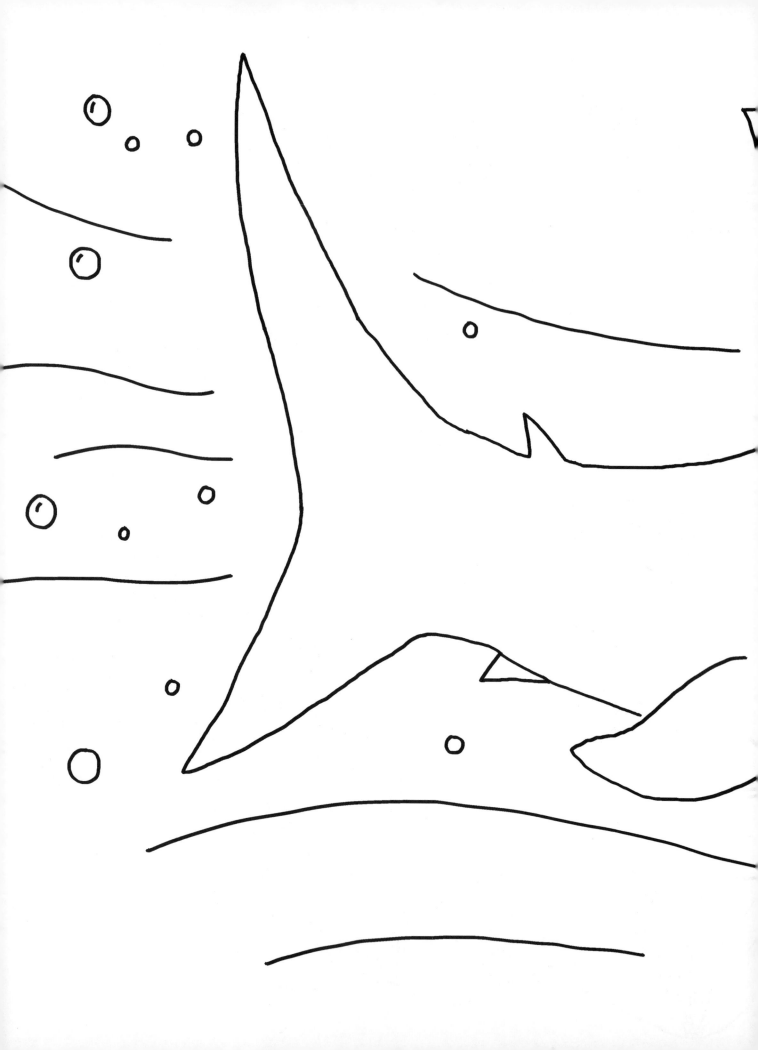

Doodle a pair of cool sunglasses onto this shark!

Connect the dots to give these lobsters some shade!

Doodle your favorite sea creatures onto this coral reef.

Give these jellyfish some fancy hats!

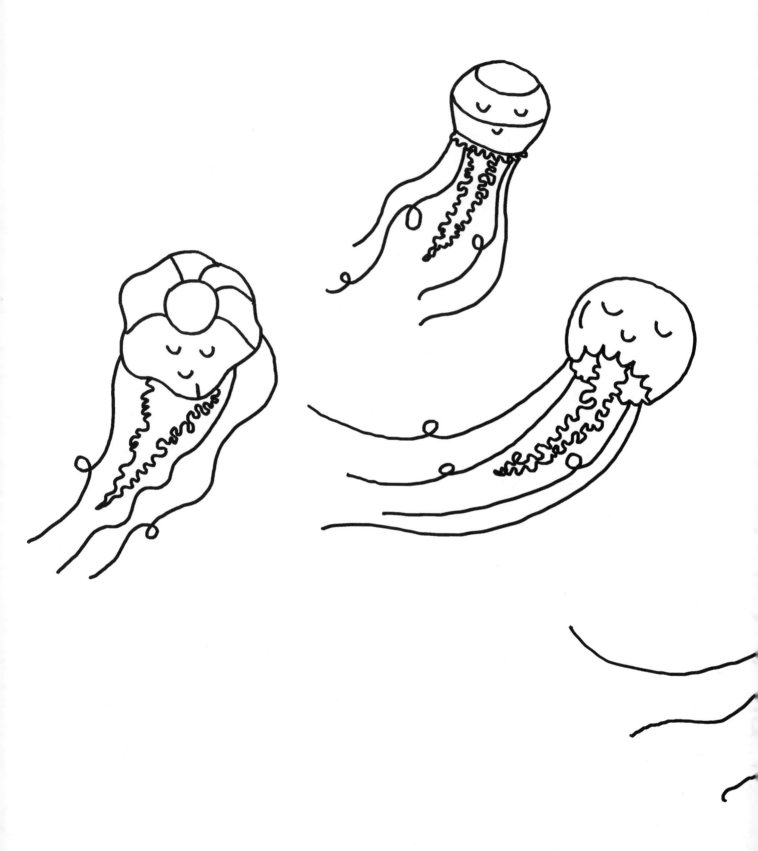